To Taryn, Kevin, Margaret and Stanley

Book design by Kristen M. Nobles.
Typeset in Guardi and Brandywine.
The illustrations in this book were rendered in acrylic washes
and colored pencil on Arches watercolor paper.
Manufactured in Hong Kong.

Library of Congress Cataloging-in-Publication Data
LaMarche, Jim.
The elves and the shoemaker / retold from the Brothers Grimm
and illustrated by Jim LaMarche.
p. cm.
Summary: A poor shoemaker becomes successful with the help of two elves
who finish his shoes during the night.
ISBN 0-8118-3477-8
[1. Fairy tales. 2. Folklore–Germany.] I. Grimm, Wilhelm, 1786–1859. II. Grimm, Jacob,
1785–1863. III. LaMarche, Jim, ill. IV. Elves and the shoemaker. English. V. Title.
PZ8.P288 El 2003
398.2'0943'02—dc21
2002015909

Distributed in Canada by Raincoast Books
9050 Shaughnessy Street, Vancouver, British Columbia V6P 6E5

10 9 8 7 6

Chronicle Books LLC
85 Second Street, San Francisco, California 94105

www.chroniclekids.com

THE ELVES AND THE SHOEMAKER

Retold from the Brothers Grimm and illustrated by Jim LaMarche

chronicle books · san francisco

here was once a good shoemaker who, through a spell of bad luck, had become very poor. Finally, he had just enough leather to make one last pair of shoes.

"Still, it is a fine piece of leather," said his wife, "as soft as butter, yet as strong as your hands."

"Tonight, dear wife, I will cut the leather," said the shoemaker, "and first thing in the morning I will sew the shoes."

The next morning, when the couple went into the workshop, they were flabbergasted by what they found. There on the worktable stood two shoes—perfectly finished, not a stitch out of place.

"But…but who? how?" sputtered the shoemaker. His wife could only stare.

Just then a dandy gentleman came into the shop. "What magnificent shoes. Please, I must try them on," he said.

The shoes fit perfectly. It was as if they had been made just for him. He was so pleased that he paid double the price. Now the shoemaker had enough money to buy leather for two more pairs of shoes.

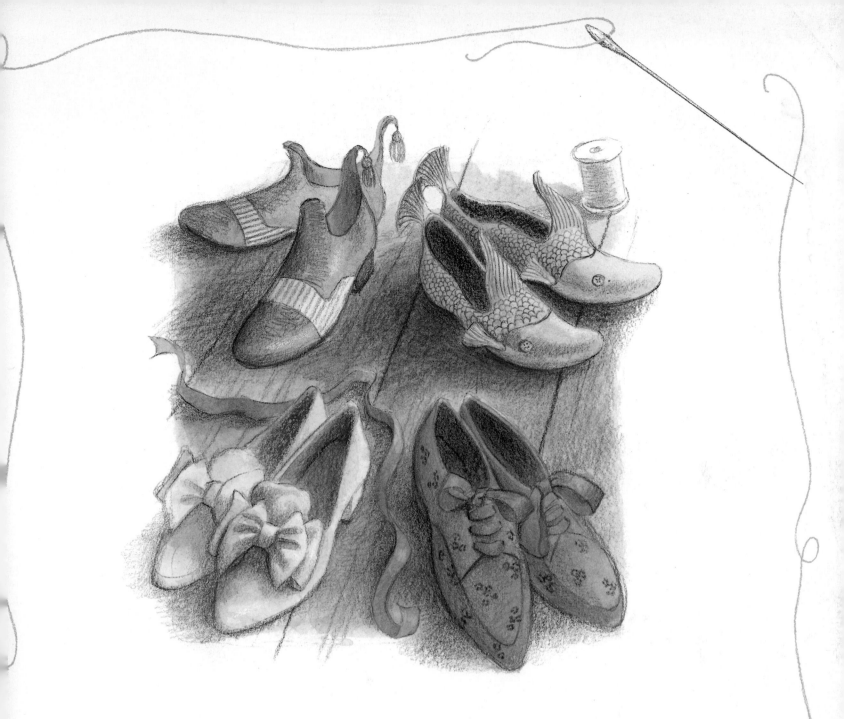

Again that evening, the shoemaker cut out the leather for the shoes and went to bed. And once again, in the morning, there were the shoes—finished! Buyers were not lacking for these either, and as before, they were so pleased, they paid double the price. Now the shoemaker had enough money to buy leather for four more pairs of shoes.

The next morning, just as before, there were the shoes already made.

On and on it went. Whatever the shoemaker cut out in the evening was finished by morning. Soon the news of the splendid shoes spread throughout the town, and the shoemaker and his wife were no longer poor.

One evening, not long before Christmas, as the shoemaker cut more leather for shoes, his wife spoke. "Dear husband, who has made us so rich? What if we were to stay up tonight and see who comes to our shop?"

The shoemaker agreed. So that night they lit a small lamp in the hall, hid behind their coats and waited. As the clock struck midnight, they heard the creak of a window and the scuttle of small feet. Peeking out from behind the coats, they saw two tiny children sneak into the workshop. They were poorly shod, and they wore only raggedy sacks for warmth.

"Elves!" the shoemaker's wife whispered.

The tiny elves tiptoed across the room and climbed up onto the table. Then, humming and whistling, they began to stitch and sew and hammer so quickly with their little fingers that the shoemaker and his wife could not believe their eyes.

The elves did not stop until all the shoes were finished and stood lined up on the table: sturdy riding boots, delicate slippers, feather-light dancing shoes and heavy clogs for work. Then the elves tiptoed out of the workshop, up the stairs and out the window.

The next morning the wife said, "The little elves have made us rich, we must give them something in return. They run around with so little on they must be freezing. I will make a warm dress, coat and pants, and knit them each a pair of stockings."

"And I shall be happy to make them each a pair of fine shoes," said the shoemaker.

They went right to work, and that evening they laid the presents on the worktable. Then, like before, they hid behind the coats and waited.

At midnight, the elves quietly slipped into the shop ready for another night's work. But instead of pieces of leather, they found the beautiful presents.

At first they were too astonished to move. Then they hugged their new warm clothes and quickly put them on.

When they were dressed, they leaped and bounced around the room, singing,

> *"Now we're elves so fine to see,*
> *no longer cobblers we will be."*

They jumped over chairs, raced around the shop and finally ran out the door. The click and clack of their new shoes echoed through the streets.

From that time on, the little elves were not seen again. But the shoemaker and his wife lived a long and happy life.

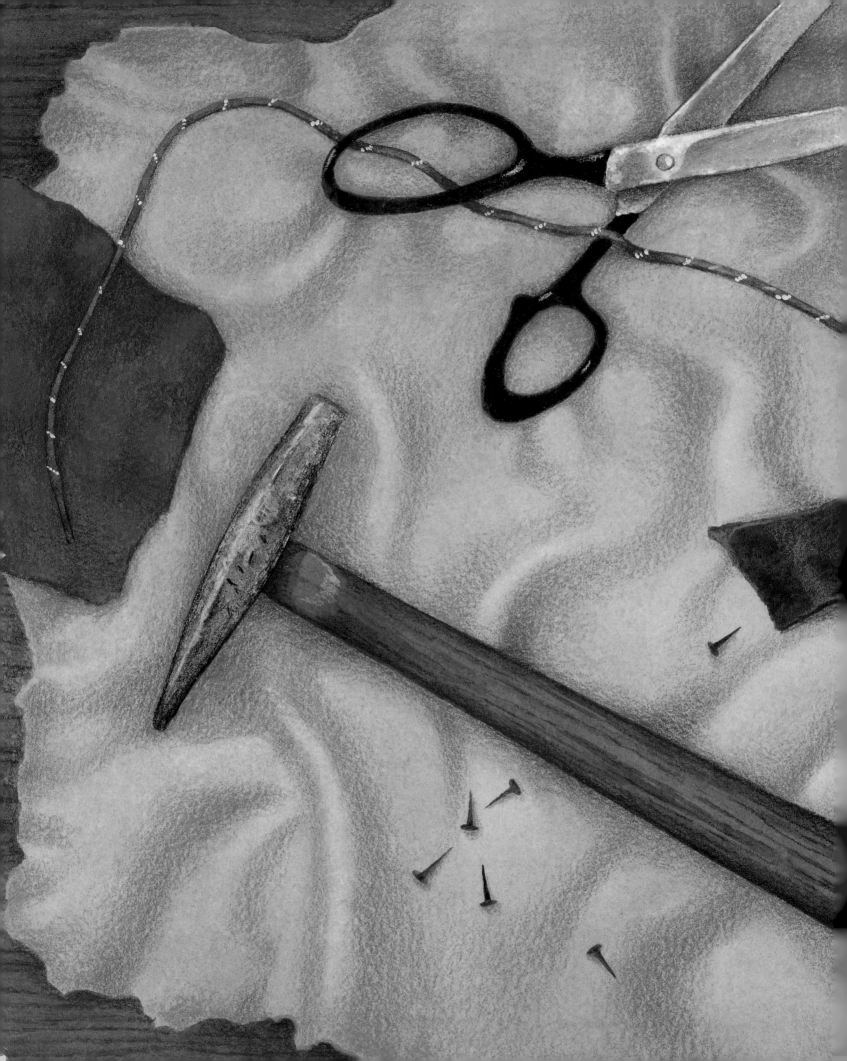